# INVASION OF THE NOSE PICKERS

## Gordon Korman

## Illustrated by Victor Vaccaro

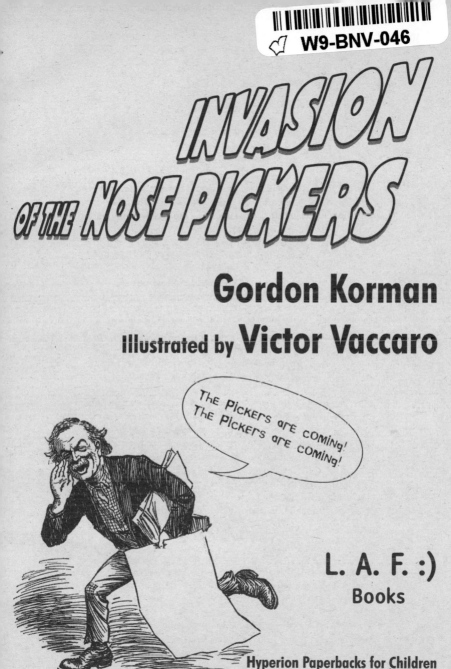

The Pickers are coming!
The Pickers are coming!

L. A. F. :)
Books

Hyperion Paperbacks for Children
New York

Printed in the United States of America
First Edition
3 5 7 9 10 8 6 4

*Library of Congress Cataloging-in-Publication Data:*
Korman, Gordon.
Invasion of the nose pickers / by Gordon Korman ;
illustrated by Victor Vaccaro.—1st ed.
p.   cm. — (L.A.F. books)
Summary: While on a fourth-grade trip to New York City,
Devin helps his friend, Stan Mflxnys, a 147-year-old alien from
the planet Pan, and other E.T.s try to locate the Humongan
who is stealing the Pants' power supply, thereby disabling the
microcomputer in Stan's nose.
ISBN 0-7868-1447-0 (pbk.)
[1. Extraterrestrial beings—Fiction. 2. Power resources—Fiction.
3. Field trips—Fiction. 4. New York (N.Y.)—Fiction. 5. Humorous
stories.] I. Vaccaro, Victor, ill. II. Title. III. Series.
PZ7.K8369 In 2001
[Fic]—dc21      00-59724

Visit www.lafbooks.com

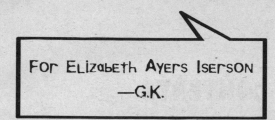

For Elizabeth Ayers Iserson
—G.K.

For Mom—V.V.

# CONTENTS

# Chapter 1
# YOU SNOOZE, YOU LOSE

---

**✳ DEVIN HUNTER'S RULES OF COOLNESS ✳**

☛ **Rule 23:** Never let yourself be pushed around by a six-year-old girl.

---

But when the six-year-old girl is my rotten sister, that's easier said than done.

Lindsay was a picture of defiance on the cafeteria bench. In each hand she clutched a peanut butter and jelly sandwich.

"Come on, Lindsay," I wheedled. "Those belong to Stan and me."

"Finders keepers, losers weepers!" she jeered at us. **"You snooze, you lose, pal."**

I'll bet my face was bright red. "You know darn well that Mom only gave them to you because Stan and I had to carry our fly-fishing poles

for the field trip tomorrow! Don't be a jerk! Hand them over!"

Obediently, she held the sandwiches out to me. Then, just as I reached out, she crammed them both into her mouth.

"Stan! Quick!"

Stan put his finger into his left nostril. Instantly, both sandwiches sprang out of Lindsay's mouth, danced a figure eight in the air, and landed in my arms.

Lindsay's eyes bulged. "What the—"

You're probably wondering how a kid could do

all that just by picking his nose. The answer is that Stan Mflxnys was no ordinary kid. He was a 147-year-old alien from the planet Pan. And he wasn't picking his nose, either. He was operating his nasal processor, a superpowered minicomputer built right into his schnoz.

"You're in trouble, Lindsay!" I snarled. "I'm telling Mom!"

"Oh, I'm *so-o-o-o* scared!" she taunted us, as we stormed away.

Back on the fourth-grade side of the cafeteria, Stan and I examined our food. The sandwiches were mangled—crushed and gross.

ABC Food—Already Been Chewed.

I sighed. "I guess we're buying lunch today."

My best friend frowned. "I, Stan, don't understand it. My nasal processor should have retrieved the sandwiches long before Lindsay could have bitten them."

**"I guess alien high technology is no match for a first grader with a bad attitude,"** I said, laughing without humor.

Stan shook his head. "I must perform a complete system diagnostic on my nasal processor."

"Sounds technical," I commented.

He nodded. "It's one of the most complex operations in Pant science."

Pants—that's what people from Pan are called. Trust me, it gets weirder. Their president is the Grand Pant. His assistants are the Under-Pants. Their top thinkers are the Smarty-Pants. Their planet is in the constellation of the Big Zipper. No lie.

I faced him. "What do you have to do?"

"I, Stan, must see how long it takes to cook a three-minute egg."

I was blown away. "What if there doesn't happen to be an egg handy?"

"Thousands of years ago, Smarty-Pants scientists were able to splice a strand of chicken DNA into the Pant gene code," Stan explained. "If there's no egg handy, we can lay our own."

Like I needed to know that. A new rule of coolness began to form in my mind: ☞ *If you can lay eggs, keep it to yourself.*

The cafeteria lady was pretty surprised when Stan told her he wanted to buy a raw egg. But when we promised we weren't going to throw it

at anybody, she held out the carton.

Stan took the egg, ducked behind the cutlery rack, and put his finger up his nose. Instantly, a bolt of lightning shot out of the other nostril, enveloping the egg in an energy field. I tapped it with a spoon. Soft-boiled to perfection.

"Did you time yourself?"

Stan nodded. "One billionth of a second."

## Chapter 2
# A GIANT FLYING SAUCER

I whistled. "Wow, that's fast!"

He looked horrified. "Fast? Devin, the standard time for a nonsneezing nasal processor should be one *trillionth* of a second."

I blew my stack. "**B i l l i o n t h !
T r i l l i o n t h !** Who cares which one it is? If you can't wait that long for a soft-boiled egg, you're a pretty impatient guy!"

"One billionth of a second is a thousand times slower than one trillionth of a second," Stan explained patiently. "It may seem like small potatoes to an Earthling, but to a Pant, it's very large potatoes indeed. It means my nasal processor is not functioning properly."

Or an
Idahoan . . .

6

That *was* serious. A nose computer was a pretty handy thing to have around. For example, tomorrow our whole fourth-grade class was going on a camping trip to Calhoun Gorge. Stan's nasal processor could fight off an angry bear, or pick nuts and berries if our food supply got pushed off a cliff. But not if it wasn't working right.

Mr. Slomin, our teacher, appeared at the entrance to the cafeteria. "Let's go, fourth grade. Lunch is over."

My stomach rumbled. For those of us with terrorists for sisters, lunch hadn't even started yet. Out of the corner of my eye I saw Stan stuffing a stack of napkins in his mouth. Pants can survive on nothing but paper, but we Earthlings require something a little more nourishing.

We were halfway up the stairs when Mr. Slomin's beeper went off. Our teacher whipped his cell phone out of his pocket and dialed. Probably not that many teachers were wired for communication like that. But Mr. Slomin was president of the Clearview UFO Society. Talk about fate. The one UFO-crazy teacher in our school just so

CaLL 1-555-UFO-NUTS

happened to get a visitor from the other side of the galaxy in his class. Luckily, Mr. Slomin never quite realized he had an actual alien right under his nose.

"Slomin, here!" He was all business. "Uh-huh . . . uh-uh . . ." Suddenly, his eyes bulged. ***"A giant flying saucer heading for New York?!"***

He took the stairs three at a time back to the classroom. We had to scramble to keep up. "Hurry! Hurry!" he called back at us. "An alien spaceship just landed in New York harbor!"

It was amazing how fast Mr. Slomin turned our little classroom into UFO central. In no time at all, two UFO-spotters from New Jersey had faxed over a sketch of the spaceship, and Mr. Slomin had it up on the overhead projector. The teacher had his cell phone against one ear, and the regular phone against the other. On his belt, the beeper was going crazy.

I examined the sketch on the screen. It was a flying saucer, all right. A handful of dark bubbles on top gave the ship the appearance of a giant chocolate-chip cookie.

"Pssst," I whispered to Stan. "Is it one of yours?" There had been a lot of Pant ships in orbit lately. But they were usually careful not to be noticed.

"Negative," Stan replied, frowning. "But my nasal processor indicates that it's a perfect match for a Humongan ship."

"Humongan?" I repeated, shocked. "You

mean there are *two* kinds of aliens coming to Earth now?"

He scratched his head. "Humongans are two-hundred-foot-tall green robots—"

"What?" My blood ran cold. I thought about

☛ **Rule 51:** Sometimes it's better to be totally clueless than to know what's really going on.

"Don't worry," Stan soothed. "There's no way any creature as large as a Humongan could visit a crowded Earth city without being noticed. I, Stan, believe this is a hoax."

I allowed myself to breathe a little easier. Mr. Slomin and his UFO buddies were kind of a flaky bunch. Maybe Stan was right.

By the end of the day, no one besides the New Jersey UFO-spotters had seen any spaceship. The Air Force just laughed when Mr. Slomin asked them to declare a national emergency. Even the Secret Service phoned to order Mr. Slomin to stop faxing the president that picture of a chocolate-chip cookie.

"Fools!" croaked Mr. Slomin. "When are they going to realize that UFO safety is the greatest challenge facing our planet?"

I thought it was PERSONAL hYGIENE.

The bell rang. Thanks to that UFO scare, we had done nothing all afternoon. And because tomorrow was the field trip, there couldn't be any homework either. High fives were flying everywhere as we got our jackets. Stan held up his hand but nobody slapped it. ☞ **Rule 67:** When you spend half your life with a finger up your nose, nobody wants to high-five you.

## Chapter 3

# COMING APART AT THE SEAMS

As soon as we got home, I made a point of ratting out Lindsay. "She did it on purpose, Mom!" I complained. "She ruined our lunches in front of the whole school! We're starving!"

"Inaccurate," Stan corrected. "I, Stan, have enjoyed a feast of succulent cafeteria napkins, with a side order of paper towels from the upstairs boys' bathroom. I even had a nip of my social studies textbook as a snack."

"Oh, Stan, you kill me!" Mom laughed. She glared at me. "Why can't you have a sense of humor about this, like Stan?"

*He isn't joking*! I wanted to tell her. But I couldn't blow Stan's cover.

"He's lucky enough to be an only child," I grumbled. "It isn't *his* sister who's turned into Godzilla Junior."

My mother sighed. "I'm sorry, Devin. I'm afraid your sister is just going through a phase right now. Six can be a very difficult age."

I thOUght shE was MOrE LiKE Darth VadEr with a tOUch OF LOrd VOLdEMOrt.

I was still griping about it when Stan and I went upstairs to the room we shared. Stan had started out as my buddy for the National Student Exchange Program. The program was over, but Stan had gotten special permission to stay longer. So he lived with us.

"If I pulled a stunt like that, I'd be grounded for a year!" I complained. "Mom and Dad let Lindsay get away with everything! She's their little darling. 'Just a phase!' What a crock!"

"I, Stan, disagree. Even Pants of the highest drawer go through a similar childhood phase at age sixty-five or so. It's called the 'phase of the knotted undergarments.'"

I frowned. "Why do they call it that?"

He shrugged. "It's when all Pants seem to

have their knickers in a twist. But because even the youngest Diaper-Pants have nasal processors, it's much more dangerous than an Earthling phase. After all, a temper tantrum with a nasal processor could knock down a building, or cause a tidal wave, or . . ."

He kept on talking, but I didn't hear a word he said. I was staring at his schnoz, which was suddenly *glowing*!

"Stan, are you all right?" I asked anxiously. "You look like Rudolph the Red-Nosed Reindeer!"

"My nose is illuminated?" Stan gasped. "This could be a Stitch-in-Time distress call coming in on an infrared frequency!" He looked at me seriously. "Pants can only use this frequency when they're truly coming apart at the seams!"

HELP! CALL a tailor!

He put a finger up his nose. "This is Agent Mflxnys on Earth responding to your call. Please identify yourself! . . . There's too much interference! I, Stan, cannot hear you. . . ."

☞ **Rule 13**: In a crisis, don't just sit there; DO something!

Hey, I'd been hanging around Stan long enough to learn a few nose-computer tricks myself. I yanked the cable wire out of my small TV and stuffed the end into Stan's free nostril. Instantly, the set clicked on.

I could hardly see anything at first. The picture was flipping like crazy. But Stan fiddled with the cable, and the image stabilized.

"Greetings, Agent Mflxnys," came a voice.

Don't worry. Stan wasn't a galactic spy or

anything like that. He was a travel agent. Pants are the greatest tourists in the galaxy. They work two weeks per year and go on vacation for the other fifty.

Stan gawked at the small screen. "Devin," he hissed at me, "do you have any idea who that is?"

I shook my head. I didn't want to hurt Stan's feelings, but most Pants kind of look alike to me. They've all got crew cuts and thick glasses that make their eyes look like fried eggs. They wear white dress shirts and black polka-dot ties. Face it; they're a bunch of interstellar dweebs.

"That's the head Smarty-Pant!" Stan whispered in awe. "Only the Under-Pants and the Grand Pant himself have more authority on Pan!"

HE PUT ThE 'GEE!' IN GENIUS.

Out loud he said, "Mr. Know-It-All! What an honor! I, Stan, assumed you'd be busy thinking on a fine day like today."

"There's no time for that now!" Mr. Know-It-All stormed, his tie flopping to and fro as he shook with anxiety. "Don't you realize what's happening here? Haven't you heard?"

Stan and I just stared at the TV. A wild scene was going on behind the head Smarty-Pant. Dozens of dweebs were running around, babbling. A blizzard of papers filled the air, as files were frantically emptied. Fried-egg eyes were wide with horror. Fingers bobbed in and out of noses like little jackhammers. It looked like Nose Picker Headquarters under siege.

"The whole planet's on high alert!" howled

Mr. Know-It-All. "The Grand Pant has given the order to fasten the Big Zipper! Every button, snap, and drawstring is tight as a drum!"

"But why?" asked Stan.

"Something," croaked the frazzled dweeb on the screen, "has been sucking all the power out of the Crease."

The Crease!

Is there an echo in here?

# Chapter 4
# CREASE PIRATES

Stan had told me about the Crease once. It's a little hard for us Earthlings to understand, but here goes.

There's a crease in the fabric of the universe. Through it flows a limitless supply of energy. That's where Pants get the power for their spaceships, their nasal processors, and almost everything on Pan.

"This is terrible, Devin!" Stan whispered to me. "Imagine Earth with dry oil wells, dead electricity, and no sun for solar energy. That would be like Pan without the Crease!"

What?! NO TV?!

I snapped my fingers. "That must be why your nose computer couldn't get those

19

sandwiches away from Lindsay in time."

"We've switched all vital systems to our backup utility—Neptunian marathon gerbils on a wheel," Mr. Know-It-All reported grimly. "But they can't keep running forever. How about you, Agent Mflxnys? What can you tell me from your end?"

"*My* end?" My exchange buddy was confused. "I, Stan, have been here on Earth the whole time."

"Exactly," said the head Smarty-Pant. "That's where the energy theft is coming from. Something on Earth is sucking power out of the Crease."

"On *Earth*?!" cried Stan in disbelief. "But that's impossible! This is a Q-class world! Earth isn't advanced enough to know the Crease even exists! There's no technology here that could tap into the Crease."

Mr. Know-It-All looked angry. "My best thinkers pinpointed the problem. It was confirmed by a crack team of ponderers. And I personally confirmed the confirmation. Are you suggesting that we, the Smarty-Pants, are— dumb?"

"No!" Stan gasped. No Pant would ever say anything bad about the Smarty-Pants.

NO . . . JUST INTELLECTUALLY CHALLENGED.

All at once, it hit me. "The spaceship!" I turned to Stan. "Mr. Slomin's UFO buddies thought they saw a spaceship heading for New York last night. That must be who's doing this! The—what did you call them?—Humongans!"

"Sir!" my exchange buddy piped up. "I, Stan,

21

have reason to believe that a Humongan ship has landed here recently. Humongans would be capable of tapping into the Crease, wouldn't they?"

"Unlikely," Mr. Know-It-All replied. "Humongans are one of the most reasonable and level-headed species in the galaxy. Why would they become Crease pirates?"

"I, Stan, promise to track them down and ask them."

"It's too late for that. The Grand Pant has made his decision. While Pan still has enough power left for space travel, we must invade Earth."

I thought my eyes would pop clean out of their sockets. "**Invade** *Earth*? But that's no fair! We never did anything to the Crease!"

"The invasion force will need to devote full power to their engines," Mr. Know-It-All told Stan. "That means their navigation computers will be shut off. Your job, Agent Mflxnys, will be to direct the fleet to Earth."

"Don't do it, Stan!" I pleaded.

But Stan stood at rigid attention. "You can count on me, sir! I, Stan, will not let the waistband droop!"

I couldn't believe it! Stan Mflxnys—my best friend—was selling us out!

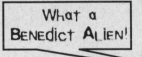

What a BENEDICT ALIEN!

## Chapter 5

# LOWER EAST HOOLA MOOLA

Stan removed his finger. The TV cable dropped to the carpet.

"You rotten, low-down traitor!" I cried accusingly. "I welcomed you like a member of the family! I fed you all the best newspapers and catalogs and phone books! I taught you my rules of coolness! **And *this* is how you repay me— by giving up Earth to an army of cosmo-nerds!"**

"But, Devin," Stan replied with a wink of one fried-egg eye. "I, Stan, promised to guide the invasion force *to* Earth. But I never mentioned *where* on Earth I'd guide them."

We ran to the globe that stood in the corner of the den. A few turns and then . . .

"Right here," said Stan. "Perfect."

He was pointing at the island of Lower East Hoola Moola, a tiny speck right smack-dab in the middle of the vast Pacific Ocean. There was nothing within a thousand miles of it in any direction.

"Won't they just move on when they realize they're in the wrong place?" I asked.

"Of course," said Stan. "But with their navigation computers off-line, that could take days.

Which gives us the time we need to track down the Humongans and straighten out this business with the Crease."

☛ **Rule 27:** Give credit where credit is due.

"Mflxnys, you're a genius," I assured him. "Quick, call that Know-It-All guy back."

I could tell the power drain was getting bad. While Stan was transmitting the coordinates, his nose computer made a whinnying sound like an old car trying to start on a cold morning.

"There's no doubt about it," he said sadly.

WHIRRRR WHIRR WHIRR

BATTERY

"We're in the middle of a full-blown Crease emergency. That's the second scariest thing that could happen to Pantkind. Only a factory defect in the Big Zipper could be more of a crisis."

"Look on the bright side," I coaxed. "At least Mr. Know-It-All was enough of a sucker to believe those fake coordinates. I'd love to see the look on his face when he winds up in Lower East Hoola Moola. What a dummy!"

"Devin!" Stan scolded me. "You're talking about the greatest mind on Pan! To become the head Smarty-Pant, you have to add up all the numbers in the universe without using a calculator or counting on your fingers! You have to do crossword puzzles in *pen*, and know the square root of a jar of peanut butter! You have to understand why the Jewish holidays always start at sundown the night before! It's *hard*!"

"Sheesh, sorry," I mumbled. ☛ **Rule 42:** Never make fun of your friend's friends.

# Chapter 6

# THE DIFFERENCE BETWEEN A GORGE AND NEW YORK CITY

The next morning, Lindsay went ballistic because she couldn't go on the camping trip with Stan and me.

"But you're only in first grade," my father explained reasonably. "When you're older, your class will go on exactly the same trip. Everybody does."

"Good. Then I'll go now and miss it later," she snarled.

"You'll just have to be patient," Mom told her gently.

*"No-fair-no-fair-no-fair-no-fair-no-fair!!"*

Dad drove us to school since we had our heavy duffel bags to carry. All the way there, he lectured us on how we

I WONDER IF SHE THINKS IT'S FAIR?

had to be extra understanding of Lindsay because of the difficult phase she was going through.

"I don't know, Dad. Are you sure it's a real phase?" I asked. "When I look at Lindsay, all I see is a rotten kid pitching a fit."

Actually, I was pretty close to pitching a fit of my own that morning. Think about it. An alien invasion force was on its way to Earth. That makes it pretty tough to get psyched about your fourth-grade camping trip.

I leaned over to Stan. "How are we going to find those Humongans when they're in New York, and we're at Calhoun Gorge?"

"I, Stan, am working on it." My exchange buddy's finger was buried deep in his nostril. He looked strained, probably because he was low on power.

We pulled up in front of the school, and Dad helped us load our duffel bags onto the bus. There was an anxious buzz among the other kids assembled on the sidewalk.

"What's going on?" I asked Calista Bernstein.

"I think there might be a problem with our trip," she told me nervously.

Mr. Slomin stood at the front of the line, rifling through our itinerary. He was gawking from sheet to sheet, totally bewildered. "This is impossible!" he cried. "We're supposed to be going to Calhoun Gorge! This schedule is for a visit to New York City!"

My head whipped around to stare at Stan. He flashed me the "index-fingers-up" sign, which was kind of like thumbs-up for Pants.

Our bus driver, Mrs. Ford, was also confused. "My directions are for New York, too. Are you sure the plan wasn't changed?"

I thought Mr. Slomin was going to blow a gasket. "On the very morning of the trip? Without telling the teacher?"

Mr. Slomin even called the tour company on his cell phone. But when I saw Stan duck behind a bush with his finger up his nose, I already knew what their answer was going to be.

"What do you mean we were *always* going to New York?" the teacher howled. "I planned this trip myself! I've got twenty-five kids with sleeping bags and hiking boots and bug spray! We've been learning fly-fishing for three weeks! Where are we supposed to do that? In the city sewer system? . . . No, I won't hold! . . ."

> Maybe theyll catch some of those mutant alligators.

Eventually, the principal himself came out to ask why we were standing around instead of loading the bus.

"Well, uh—" stammered Mr. Slomin. You could tell he wanted to explain our problem, but he was afraid to look like an idiot in front of Dr. Bickleford. Thanks to Stan's nose computer, there wasn't the slightest clue anywhere that this had ever been a trip to Calhoun Gorge. I thought of a new rule of coolness for Mr. Slomin:

☛ Never let your boss think you don't know the difference between a gorge and New York City.

"Broadway, here we come," the teacher declared finally. "Everybody onto the bus."

# Chapter 7
# CAMPING IN CENTRAL PARK

The drive to New York took four hours, just about the same as Calhoun Gorge. Then, right outside the city, we got stuck in the biggest traffic jam I've ever seen.

Stan loved it. Pants have some pretty bizarre tastes. He was staring out the window, mesmerized by the scene all around us. It was like a giant parking lot. **"This is fantastic,"** he raved. **"Sitting for hours, yet barely moving!** It's almost as thrilling as going to the dentist!"

"We're not here to enjoy the traffic," I reminded him in a low voice. "How are we going to find the Humongans?"

Stan shrugged. "How difficult can it be to locate a two-hundred-foot green robot? It can't exactly blend into the scenery, you know. Oh, look. That cement mixer just cut us off. What fun!"

At last, we made it through the tunnel and onto the busy streets of Manhattan. Even I have to admit it was pretty cool—pounding on the bus windows, waving at all the taxis and limos that swarmed around us, and gawking up at the tall buildings.

Stan wasn't very impressed. "You told me New York had skyscrapers."

I stared at him. "Are you kidding me? The Empire State Building alone is over a hundred stories high."

**"That wouldn't even come close to scraping the sky,"** he harrumphed. "On Pan, our tallest building, the Levi Strauss Center, is over four billion stories in height. The Designer Jeans had to run the elevator through a hyper-space shortcut or else it would take three weeks to get to the top."

Since all we had was camping equipment, our driver took us to Central Park. We stopped in a wide grassy field called the Great Lawn. Then came the hard part—setting up our tent. In no time, Tanner Phelps had somehow zipped his jacket into the zipper door. Calista was wrapped up in so much canvas that she looked like a mummy. Joey Petrillo held the stake steady for Ralph O'Malley to pound in.

Wham! Ralph swung the mallet down with crushing force onto Joey's thumb.

"Yeeeow!!"

And then Stan put his finger in his nose. With a *whoosh*, a great wind billowed from under the canvas, standing the big tent upright. Calista was demummified and launched right into the arms of a bewildered Mr. Slomin. The poles snapped smartly into place, and the stakes jumped up and hammered themselves into the ground.

We rushed to free Tanner, who was hanging by his jacket, still zipped to the front entrance flap.

There were *ooh*s and *aah*s from the class. Stan's nose computer had added a few extras to the tent, like a basketball hoop, a weather vane, and a welcome mat. A flock of city pigeons descended on the bird feeder.

I was impressed. Even at low power, the Crease sure could put on a show.

Mr. Slomin was confused, but he was still ready to take credit for what had happened—whatever *that* was.

"Uh—excellent work, people," he said approvingly, in a shaky voice. "I told you I could get this tent up."

We watched as a police car pulled up behind

the bus. A tall uniformed officer got out and approached the teacher.

"Hey, pal, what do you think you're doing? There's no camping here."

"But—but—" Poor Mr. Slomin had spent most of the day in a state of confusion, and things didn't make any more sense now. At a loss for words, he showed the officer our trip itinerary. The cop radioed the station house, and sure enough, a fourth-grade class from Clearview Elementary School had special permission to camp on the Great Lawn of Central Park for the next three days.

"Darnedest thing," the officer told Mr. Slomin. "I've been a cop here for thirty years, and no one's ever been allowed to do this. You folks must have a lot of clout. Is the governor's kid in this class or something?"

"Nope. Just a normal group of fourth graders," replied Mr. Slomin.

Plus one galactic travel agent with a magic nose, I thought.

## Chapter 8

# THE UNITED NATIONS

At the souvenir stand, everybody else bought T-shirts, key chains, hats, and stuff like that. Stan and I pooled our money and purchased a cheap pair of binoculars and an "I ♥ NY" transistor radio. During the whole two-hour bus tour, Stan scoured the city for signs of Humongans, while I listened to the radio for reports of two-hundred-foot aliens terrorizing New York.

There was nothing on the news, but maybe New Yorkers didn't get scared by alien invaders. They seemed like a pretty cool group of people to me. No one was fazed by taxis that drove ninety miles an hour and then screeched to a halt three inches behind the cars in front of them. Could it be that giant robots were no big deal either?

LOOK. MargE. It's thE aLiEn invadErs again.

I leaned over to Stan. "Any chance the Humongans are hiding inside one of those big buildings?" I whispered.

"Impossible," he replied. "My nasal processor is equipped with a Pan-tastic alien life form detector. If there are Humongans inside these structures, it will pinpoint them and alert us."

The last stop on our tour was the United Nations. By that time, Stan and I were pretty nervous. We had driven all over New York, and we still had no clue where the Humongans might be hiding. We weren't even completely sure there *were* any Humongans!

The United Nations was really cool, but today it just made me feel even more worried. When Mr. Slomin showed us the spectacular display of the flags of all 188 member countries, it only re-minded me of how much was at stake. Invaders were on their way to Earth right now. It was easy to look at Pants as a big joke because they've always got their fingers up their noses. But they had spaceships and technology that were light-years ahead of us. You bet it was scary.

The highlight of our tour was a visit to the famous General Assembly. It was a huge room set up sort of like a theater. Each country had a desk where its ambassadors and diplomats sat. I couldn't really figure out what they were voting on—catching codfish off the coast of Newfoundland, or something dull like that. I reminded myself of ☞ **Rule 39:** Just because something is boring doesn't mean it isn't important.

Suddenly, a small, slight man in brightly colored robes ran up to the podium at the front and

cried, "My friends, stop voting! I must alert you to a most horrible and beastly injustice going on in my home and native land!"

The secretary general stared at the guy. You could tell he didn't have a clue who he was. "And your country is . . . ?" he prompted.

The funny little man drew himself up to his full height and announced, "It is my honor to represent the government of Lower East Hoola Moola."

Uh-oh.

NatioNaL SYMbOl:
HOOLa HOOP.

## Chapter 9

# GENERAL PUT·ON

"Lower East *what*?" chorused a number of diplomats.

"Hoola Moola," the ambassador said with dignity. "Including Lower East Hoola Moola itself and the islands of the greater Moola archipelago. At this very moment, my people—a brave people, a proud people—are being invaded."

"Invaded?" The secretary general was shocked. "By whom?"

"Pants!" cried the ambassador. "As we speak, platoons of GI Pants are hovering over my beloved island paradise in flying tank tops! Invaders climb down from suspenders that drop from the sky! Our president is being held in Pant-cuffs!"

What a fashion victim.

Poor Stan looked like he wanted to crawl into a hole. We were so busy patting ourselves on the back for sending the invasion force to the middle of nowhere! I guess it never crossed our minds that this wasn't exactly going to be much fun for the Hoola Moolans.

I was nervous. I could just picture every country on Earth banding together to help the Hoola Moolans win back their island.

It was like watching a train wreck   you could see it coming, but you couldn't stop it.

Or could you?

I cupped my hands to my mouth. "Tell us about the invaders' weapons!" I called down.

"Devin!" Mr. Slomin scolded, horrified.

Stan looked at me in confusion.

I could see some of the delegates scanning the visitors' gallery. They could hear me!

*"What are the invaders' weapons?!"* I bellowed again.

Mr. Slomin was turning red. "Shhh!" he hissed. "You're interfering with important world affairs!"

But the Hoola Moolan ambassador answered

my question. "The Pants are unarmed," he admitted.

"Unarmed?" repeated the secretary general. "Then how have they managed to subdue your entire country?"

"With their noses," replied the ambassador.

| A NOSE KNOWS. |

There were snickers in the General Assembly.

"These are no ordinary noses!" the little man insisted, highly insulted. "They have been bewitched with special powers. To harness this

44

magic, an invader must merely insert his index finger into his nostril like so." And he actually did it, just like a Pant working his nose computer.

The United Nations erupted with laughter.

The ambassador was enraged. "Oh, so you think this is funny?" he shouted. "Let's see how amused you are after you view this videotape from the invaders!"

The lights dimmed, and a remarkable-looking Pant appeared on the big screen at the front.

Stan squeezed my shoulder hard enough to splinter the bone. **"That's General Put-On!"** he rasped in horror.

"Put-On?" I repeated. "That doesn't sound like a Pant name."

"His real name is Tnhrnys," Stan quavered. "But everyone calls him General Put-On because he puts on his trousers both legs at the same time! I, Stan, should have realized he would be selected to lead the invasion force. He's the supreme high commander of the Crease Police!"

# Chapter 10
# INSIDE OUT

"Even the Smarty-Pants are frightened of General Put-On," Stan raved, white to the ears. "He's the roughest, toughest, meanest stone-washed Pant in the galaxy!"

Stan filled me in. This Put-On guy was more than just a general. He was a planetary legend. Pant parents say to their little kids, **"Don't chew on the yellow pages or we'll tell General Put-On."** Almost like the bogeyman here on Earth! In addition to leading the Crease Police, he was the Under-Pant who oversaw teeth-gnashing and stepping on ants, the Smarty-Pant in charge of thinking up ways to break things, and a level five grandmaster at Candy Land. He *invented* frowning! According to Stan, before General Put-On, everybody smiled almost all the time.

It MUST have SEEMED LiKE TELETubbyLaNd.

I squinted at the screen. The general sat ramrod straight in the saddle atop a large feathered—

"What's with Big Bird?" I asked.

"General Put-On always rides a Rigellian fire-breathing ostrich named Monty," Stan supplied. "It's standard issue for all seventy-four-star generals."

"He doesn't look so bad," I murmured. Nobody in a polka-dot tie ever seems tough to me.

"You know the constellation of Gemini?" Stan asked.

I nodded. "The Twins."

"Well, there used to be only one guy," Stan explained, "until General Put-On got mad and rammed it with his spaceship so hard that it split into two. All because he couldn't get his parking validated. They sing songs about his temper in twenty different star systems."

The general looked like every other Pant except he wore a military helmet that magnified his fried-egg eyes into exploding suns. His white dress shirt had epaulets that extended a foot past each shoulder to fit his seventy-four stars. The ostrich burped and a shaft of flame shot out of its

mouth, roasting a nearby palm tree to ashes.

"Uh-oh," whispered Stan. "When he's in a bad mood, General Put-On feeds Monty nothing but chili with raw onions. A Rigellian fire-breathing ostrich can burn down a whole rain forest with a single hiccup."

SMOKEY BEAR says: ONLY YOU—and PEPTO-BISMOL—can prevent FOREST FIRES.

"Citizens of the Q-class planetoid known as Earth," the general began in a voice that echoed all around the United Nations. "I bring this warning from his Most Tailored majesty, the Grand Pant. If the force that is tapping energy from the Crease is not shut off by midnight on Friday, I vow to turn the planet inside out looking for it. **Now I must go and award myself some more medals.**"

Then, just before the screen went dark, General Put-On snapped to a smart salute that ended with his finger up his nostril. There were howls of laughter in the General Assembly. Diplomats were rolling in the aisles. The secretary general was doubled over. Even Mr. Slomin, who saw aliens behind every door, exclaimed, "What a ridiculous hoax! Magic noses indeed!"

I leaned over to Stan. "See? That wasn't so terrible."

Stan stared at me. "Didn't you hear General Put-On? He's going to turn the planet inside out!"

"Oh, that's just an expression," I laughed. "My mom says it whenever she can't remember where she put something—'I'll turn the whole house inside out looking for it.'"

Stan shook his head gravely. "Turning a planet inside out is General Put-On's usual search procedure."

"**You mean—**" I was horrified, "**he's actually going to turn the whole Earth inside out?**"

Stan looked sheepish. "Sorry, Devin, but it's policy."

"But what's the point of that?" I complained.

"A couple of centuries ago, a band of interstellar jewel thieves stole the Grand Pant's royal pocket stud and hid it at the core of Saturn. It was a bold plan, but the criminals weren't counting on General Put-On. To remember where they'd stashed the loot, they'd established rings around the planet. Well, the general saw through that in a minute. He merely turned Saturn inside out to get the stud back. He left the rings up as a warning: Don't try to put on Put-On."

"Yeah, but Saturn's a *gas* planet," I reminded him. "It's easy to turn inside out. Earth is—*stuff*!"

Stan nodded apologetically. "It's a lot messier with a solid world."

"He's bluffing!" I cried. "How can he do all that? Pan is practically out of power. Your nasal processors sound like old cars, and you haven't even got enough juice to turn on a navigation computer!"

"Unfortunately," Stan replied, "it takes very little energy to turn a planet inside out. Earth's

own gravity will be twisted around so that everything on the surface winds up in the middle, and
vice versa."

I couldn't see myself, but I must have turned
pale. Everything—supermarkets, hockey rinks,
the Rocky Mountains, my house, not to mention
6 billion people—would get buried under solid
rock! And talk about hot! The Earth's core was
where all that lava came from! What didn't get
squashed would get fried!

It would all happen in two days if we couldn't
solve the mystery of what was tapping the
Crease.

## Chapter 11

# THE GREAT GALACTIC
# LEDERHOSEN

From the time we opened our eyes in the morning till the time we went to sleep at night, nobody could forget that we were in the Big Apple.

At dawn we awoke to hoofbeats on the horse trails by our tent. New York society was going for its morning ride. The trucks came next, followed by the taxis. By this time, the runners, the 'bladers, and the bikers were thick on the paths, and Mr. Slomin was choosing a group of volunteers to go buy fresh bagels for our breakfast. The campfire kettle was boiling up our hot chocolate. It would have been an amazing trip, if it wasn't for the fact that Earth was in terrible danger.

Stan had a morning routine of his own—a crisp new white dress shirt (heavy starch), polka-dot tie, ten deep knee bends, and then into the woods for a system diagnostic on his nasal processor.

That day I went with him.

"A twenty-thousandth of a second," he said dejectedly, handing me the soft-boiled egg.

"That's fifty million times slower than usual. I, Stan, fear the drain on the Crease is becoming critical."

I shook my head miserably. "What are we going to *do*, Stan?"

"Our best," he replied bravely. "We Pants have an old saying: '**Do your best, for better or worsted.**'"

The first stop on our schedule that day was the Museum of Natural History. There we stood in the dinosaur gallery, looking up at the skeleton of *Tyrannosaurus rex*, when Stan elbowed me in the ribs and whispered, "I don't see what everybody is so excited about. My nasal processor indicates that this life form has been dead for over sixty million years. What do they expect it to do—sit up and beg?"

YEah!

I was mad at him. "Don't waste your nose power on dinosaur bones! We're looking for aliens, remember?"

But Stan just couldn't seem to keep his mouth shut that day. In the planetarium show next door, our whole class got kicked out because my exchange buddy was heckling the narrator.

"This universe is all wrong!" he called out. "Where's the Big Zipper? You've got triple stars as double stars, and double stars as singles! Your black holes are only dark gray! What's more, you've left out the Asteroid Belt completely! **Without the belt, what's holding up the Great Galactic Lederhosen?**"

At lunch over real Manhattan pizza, Mr. Slomin gave us a serious lecture. "We didn't come to New York so you could insult people, Mflxnys." He frowned. "In fact, I'm not sure why we came to New York at all. We were supposed to be at Calhoun Gorge. But whatever the reason, we're here now, and you're going to be polite. Is that clear?"

"Yes, Mr. Slomin," mumbled Stan, his mouth full of napkins.

After lunch, we hit F.A.O. Schwarz, the famous toy store. The place is practically alive. You can't escape the bells, sirens, whistles, buzzers, computer voices, horns, and beeps in every pitch. Why, there was even a noise coming from somewhere that sounded exactly like Stan's nose comp—

I pinched him hard enough to remove the flesh
from his bones. "Stan! That's you!"

But he was way ahead of me. His finger was
buried up there to the second knuckle.

"Devin!" he hissed excitedly. "My Pan-tastic
alien life form detector has located an alien!"

"A Humongan?" I asked anxiously. I looked
around like I was expecting to see a two-
hundred-foot robot standing there in the electric-
train department.

Stan wiggled his finger. "I, Stan, can't tell. The signal is very faint."

Suddenly, wisps of smoke began to curl out of Stan's ears. I grabbed him by the elbow and yanked his finger down. "Careful! You're starting to overload!"

DOESN'T HE SEE THE NO SMOKING SIGN?

"Oh, yuck!" Calista cried from across the store. "Stan's picking his nose again! And Devin's helping!"

We ignored her.

"I, Stan, must find a power booster for my alien life form detector!" Stan exclaimed urgently. "Quick, before the alien gets away!"

I took in our surroundings. We were in the middle of a toy store. It wasn't exactly Clearview Light and Power Company.

And then it came to me. I yanked a tiny locomotive out of the setup on the counter. I flipped it open, fished out a triple-A battery, and handed it to Stan. He grabbed it and shoved it, anode-first, up his nose.

## Chapter 12
# BATTERIES NOT INCLUDED

"Oh, that's better." The bottom of the battery stuck out of his nostril. It bobbed up and down as he talked. "The signal is quite close. And—" He frowned. "Devin, quick—another battery."

I was astonished. "What happened to that one?"

"It's used up."

"So *fast*?"

"Devin, this is the power of the *Crease* we're replacing," he explained. "To get my nasal processor up to full speed for even a few minutes, we would need at least seventeen thousand, eight hundred twenty-six and a half of those batteries."

"Seventeen *thousand*?" I echoed.

"Give or take eight hundred twenty-six and a half," he added.

That's a LOT of Energizer Bunnies.

"Listen, Stan. Even if we could find that many batteries, so what? We have to chase down aliens! Can you carry seventeen thousand batteries? I can't."

"Hmmm. I see your point," he said thoughtfully. "However, I, Stan, know of a Pant who is in New York right now. He might be able to help us."

"Is he really strong?" I asked.

My exchange buddy nodded. **"His name is Stncldnys, but here on Earth he's known as Stone Cold Steve Austin."**

"Stone Cold Steve Austin?" I repeated. "From the WWF? *He's* an alien?"

Stan chuckled. "You didn't think a mere Earthling could wrestle like that, did you?"

I'll never get used to finding out how many famous people are actually Pants posing as Earthlings. When you think about it, it makes perfect sense. They have nose computers, so whatever they do, they're bound to be better at it than us humans. So, sure, they get famous. Shakespeare, Jerry Springer, even Michael Jordan—all Pants. And now Stone Cold Steve Austin.

That EXPLaINS it!

I handed Stan a battery. "Phone him up."

Stan put the triple-A in one nostril and his finger in the other. "Calling Stncldnys the Crushingly Powerful. This is Agent Mflxnys. Oh, sure. I'll hold." To me he whispered, "He's busy stomping someone."

"Maybe he's using his famous end move, the

Stone Cold stunner," I said reverently. "Here, take another battery."

"Stncldnys, this is an emergency," Stan said when the wrestler came back on line. "Meet me in front of F.A.O. Schwarz on Fifth Avenue in ten minutes." He tossed aside another dead battery. "He's on his way."

It was bizarre to think of a dweeb like Stan barking orders at the great Stone Cold Steve Austin. I had to remind myself that Stan was Pan's head travel agent on Earth, and that made him Stone Cold's boss. Weird, huh?

Then it was time to sneak away from the group to visit Stan's, *ahem*, employee. Mr. Slomin was so afraid of losing somebody in the big city that he was constantly counting heads. To escape his watchful eye, we were going to have to get low.

We crawled along the floor until we made it to the coolest toy in the whole place—a miniature Porsche Carrera, silver gray, with a real electric engine. We slipped into the seats—Corinthian leather. And before I knew it, Stan was steering us toward the exit.

"Don't hit anything!" I rasped. "The price tag says eleven thousand dollars!"

PEANUTS!

I kept my eye on the rearview mirror. When Mr. Slomin disappeared behind the giant model of the Alps in the display for Ski Chalet Barbie, we ditched the car and ran outside.

Perfect timing. A limo pulled up and out stepped Stone Cold Steve Austin himself. He was even bigger than I expected. Huge muscles bulged through his black *Austin 3:16* T-shirt. And what came out of the mouth of the most famous wrestler of all time?

"Greetings, Agent Mflxnys. May the Crease be with you."

## Chapter 13
# FACE·TO·FACE WITH AN ALIEN

"Ah, yes, the Crease," Stan told Stone Cold Steve Austin. "That's the problem, Stncldnys. The Crease isn't going to be with any of us pretty soon."

He filled the wrestler in on the mysterious power drain.

Stone Cold nodded understandingly. "I noticed my nasal processor hasn't been working very well," he reported. "Usually, all it takes is a touch of my nostril and I've got my opponent flat on the mat, pinned. But lately, I've actually had to *fight* these people—which is no problem. But it makes you so sweaty!"

I didn't like to interrupt, but we needed to get

this show on the road if we were going to catch the alien. "Mr. Austin, we need seventeen thousand batteries, but we're not strong enough to carry them. Are you?"

"Triple-A's?" he asked, all business.

I nodded. **"Nostril size."**

He flexed his arm muscles. I almost felt a wind from the motion.

So we got the batteries. I know that sounds too simple. But when you're with Stone Cold Steve Austin, nobody gives you a hard time about things. He just signed an autograph for the security guard and asked to go to the warehouse. And they left us alone in there!

Stan and Stone Cold each took a battery to get started, and stuffed them into their nasal processors. That gave them enough power to send thousands of triple-A's floating off the warehouse shelves that stretched up forty feet high.

It was something to see! Giant rolls of masking tape soared into the air, wrapping the batteries end to end. Pretty soon, 17,856 single units had been turned into a cable of DC power over eight football fields long.

Stone Cold wrapped the whole thing into a giant coil, which he slung over his massive shoulders.

"Okay," he said, grunting under the strain of the weight. "Let's move out."

"Not so fast," I said quickly. "We can't just take these batteries. That's stealing!"

"Devin!" Stan was shocked. "We would never do that! We left an interstellar payment voucher backed up by the Grand Pant himself and our planetary bank, the Pocket."

I looked around for it. "Where?"

Stan chuckled. "Since Earth doesn't know that Pan exists, it was necessary for us to make the voucher invisible so as not to interfere with Earth's normal development. But you can rest assured that it's there, good as gold. You have my word as a Pant of the Second Drawer from the Top. Right, Stncldnys?"

"That's the bottom line," rumbled the big wrestler, "'cause Stone Cold said so!"

☛ **Rule 61:** Never argue with anyone who could snap your neck with a hiccup.

I was afraid that the alien might have buzzed off while we were setting up our power station. But when Stan plugged in the battery cable, his Pan-tastic alien life form detector started beeping again.

"This way!" cried Stan, pointing to a rear exit from the warehouse.

On the dead run, he headed out the door, with Stone Cold Steve Austin loping along behind him, lugging the seventeen thousand triple-A's. I brought up the rear. I was anxious to get out of there before someone accused me of Grand Theft Batteries.

As we ran down the narrow alley, I could hear Stan's nose beeping faster and faster. We were getting close! A feeling of dread started to grip at my chest. Were we about to come face-to-face with a two-hundred-foot robot? That was an alien monster even Stone Cold couldn't handle.

"Aha!" I heard Stan yell.

I rounded the corner and stopped dead in my tracks. There, trapped between the two Pants, a broken basket full of half-rotten apples, and the side of the building, sat a thin, gray—

"A *rat*?" I exclaimed.

# Chapter 14
# THE CHEESY WAY GALAXY

"Hey, buddy, who are you calling a rat?" the long-tailed creature snapped at me. **"I'm a *Ra'at* from the planet Rodentia Alpha in the Cheesy Way galaxy.** Show some respect."

"An intergalactic traveler!" exclaimed Stan. "What are you doing on Earth?"

"Isn't it obvious?" The Ra'at sunk his sharp teeth into the core of a Granny Smith near the top of the basket. "I'm getting my piece of the Big Apple."

I couldn't believe it! He wasn't a Humongan! He wasn't a Pant! How many different kinds of aliens were there on Earth? The next time I saw a mosquito, would it be a real bug, or a guy from Jupiter or something?

"Have you been messing with the Crease?" I demanded.

The Rodentian traveler was highly insulted. "Listen, pal, we Ra'ats have two directives we always follow. One: never fool around with another species' power source; and two: don't let your tail dangle too close to the paper shredder."

I was really upset. "You mean we got the wrong guy? Someone *else* is tapping the Crease?"

The Ra'at choked on an apple seed. "Someone's tapping the Crease? Man, I gotta get out of here before the Grand Pant sends General Put-On to turn the whole place inside out!"

He tried to scurry off, but Stone Cold delicately grabbed him by the tail.

"Hey, musclehead, what's the big idea?" he complained. "You're violating the Galactic Charter on the Treatment of Rodents!"

**"Nobody likes a Ra'at who deserts a sinking ship,"** the big wrestler shot back.

"Earth is in big trouble," I informed the Rodentian. "General Put-On is already here. If you can do anything to help us—"

Stan had his finger up his nose. "Unlikely, Devin. My nasal processor indicates that Ra'ats are not known to have any special talents."

The intergalactic visitor was appalled. "Are you kidding? You'll never find a more talented life form than us Ra'ats! Dogs may be man's best friend on Earth, but we Ra'ats are best friend to species on thirty-six different planets, moons, asteroids, floating rocks, and clouds of space dust. Tie our tails together and you've got a pair of fur earmuffs that can sing to you in two-part harmony. When it comes to infesting, we're number three in the universe, after *Cockroachus maximus* and *Termitus munchus*. And we're unmatched anywhere when it comes to cheating at Candy Land."

Now, that's a rESUMé.

"Hold it!" I turned to Stan. "Didn't you say General Put-On likes to play Candy Land?"

"He's a level-five grand master," Stan replied. "He's never lost. His fireplace at home is over six miles long so he has room on the mantel for all his trophies."

"Let me at him," the Ra'at urged. "He's met his match with Ra'at A. Tooey—**king of the Lollipop Woods, master of the Gumdrop Pass, lord of the Molasses Swamp**. Where is he?"

"The island of Lower East Hoola Moola," I supplied.

Ra'at A. Tooey was surprised. "He'll never find any decent Candy Land competition way out there. They've got nothing but palm trees and tiki huts."

"And one Ra'at," I decided. "If you can get him involved in a long Candy Land tournament, that might buy us some more time to find out

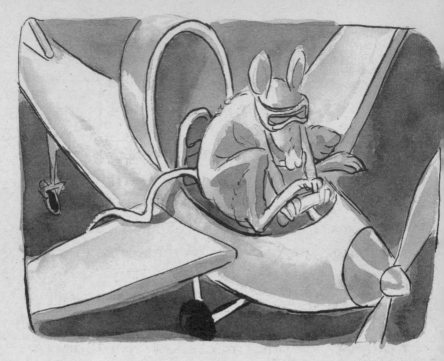

who's been messing with the Crease." I frowned.
"But how can we fly you all the way to Hoola
Moola?"

Stone Cold Steve Austin hefted the coils of
batteries around his shoulders. "Kid, we've got
*power*."

We went back into the F.A.O. Schwarz warehouse. Stan picked out a small remote control
plane and opened the cockpit bubble. Ra'at A.
Tooey crawled behind the controls and plucked a
pair of goggles off the little plastic pilot. Stan held

the engine up to his free nostril and snorted. The toy plane's propellers roared to life.

"How will we know if he makes it?" I asked Stan over the noise.

"I, Stan, have established a nose-to-nose cone communications link with the aircraft," my exchange buddy replied.

"It's in the bag!" the Rodentian called to us. "There are two things you can always count on with us Ra'ats: We never give up, and we always find a way to get in through your toilet pipes."

*Zoom!!* The small plane rocketed out of the warehouse and disappeared in the glare of the sun.

> It's a bird.
> It's a PLANE.
> It's a . . . rat?

Stan removed the end of the power cord from his nose. "Dead," he announced. "I, Stan, was forced to inject full energy into the plane's engine for the long trip to Lower East Hoola Moola."

Stone Cold Steve Austin had a Wrestlemania event in New Jersey that night. So he wished us luck and went to get ready. Stan and I snuck out of the warehouse back into F.A.O. Schwarz.

My head was spinning. Earth's safety depended

on a rat—excuse me, a Ra'at—flying halfway around the world in a toy plane to challenge an alien general to a game meant for six-year-olds.

Just when I thought things couldn't possibly get any scarier, I saw him standing in the games department, madder than fire. Mr. Slomin.

*"Where-have-you-been-we've-been-waiting-for-over-an-hour-we've-missed-our-matinée-of-*The-Lion-King-*thanks-to-you-two-immature-irrespon-sible-thoughtless . . ."*

It didn't end. As he yelled at us, the wind from his tantrum blew my hair into my eyes. I thought about how unfair all this was. Everything we'd done had been to try to save Earth. But how could we ever explain that to Mr. Slomin? UFO spotter or not, he'd think we were nuts.

**"New York is *over* for you two!"** he bawled at us. "As of this minute, *you're grounded!*"

Stan and I exchanged a look of sheer agony. If Ra'at A. Tooey couldn't make it to Lower East Hoola Moola, "grounded" was going to take on a whole new meaning.

## Chapter 15

# THE TIMES SQUARE
# JUMBOTRON

☛ **Rule 66:** Nothing can drive you crazy faster than sitting around twiddling your thumbs when there's important work to be done.

That night the whole class got to go to the Hard Rock Café for dinner and then on to Madison Square Garden for a New York Knicks game against the L.A. Lakers. Being grounded, Stan and I had to stay in the tent, eating instant macaroni over the campfire with Mr. Slomin. He was even madder at us than before because he was missing a great dinner and the game, while Mrs. Ford, the bus driver, got to use his ticket.

"Oh, it's okay, Mr. Slomin," I tried to assure him. "Stan and I can look after ourselves. We've learned our lesson now. If you take a taxi, you can probably catch the second half of the game."

"This never would have happened at Calhoun Gorge," the teacher muttered, not even answering me. "Now *that* would have been a field trip. I still can't figure out why we didn't go."

At 10:30 P.M., Mrs. Ford and the class came back, raving about "the most fun we've ever had in our lives." That got Mr. Slomin so riled up he couldn't sleep. So much for our plan to sneak away and continue the search for Humongans. Stan and I both dozed off while our teacher was still tossing and turning, muttering under his breath.

It was the middle of the night when Stan's crazed voice jarred me awake.

"Quick!" he exclaimed. "Get the mousetrap!"

I turned around in my bedroll. Stan was fast asleep, but his nose was blinking red, blue, red, blue. . . .

"We've got rats! Call an exterminator!"

I shook him. "Stan, shhhh! You're having a nightmare!"

He sat up and put a finger to his nose.

"Negative, Devin," he whispered. "I, Stan, am receiving a live transmission from the nose-to-nosecone communications link. Since my nasal processor was in 'sleep' mode, the signal was automatically relayed to my mouth."

"You mean—" I began.

He nodded. "Ra'at A. Tooey has reached the island of Lower East Hoola Moola. Those were the cries of the GI Pants as he infested their campsite."

Careful not to wake our classmates and our teacher, who was finally asleep, we crept out of the tent. I took my transistor radio and inserted the tip of the antenna into Stan's nose.

What a racket. There was a whole lot of crashing and shrieking going on, along with shouts of, "Get the broom!" and "What do you mean you left the rat poison on Alpha Centauri?"

"What a bunch of wimps," I commented. "You'd think they'd never seen a Ra'at before."

"Oh, they have," Stan assured me. "But it's very hard to tell the difference between a Ra'at and just a plain rat."

At that very moment, Ra'at A. Tooey bellowed, "I'll bet five brown apple cores and half a pack of Tic Tacs that there isn't a soldier in this army who's Pant enough to beat me at Candy Land!"

THEM'S FIGHTIN' WORDS!

"And if you win?" came a voice.

Sudden silence fell.

"The general!" Stan hissed. "Who else could quiet a crowd of soldiers when there's a rat in the barracks?"

"If I win," said the Ra'at, "you have to promise not to turn Earth inside out."

"General, we can't agree to that!" urged a GI Pant. "We could lose our only way to find the Crease Pirates!"

General Put-On chuckled. "I've never lost anything in my entire life—not my spaceship keys, not my lunch, not even my baby teeth. And certainly not a game of Candy Land. Mr. Ra'at, I accept your challenge. **May the best life form win.**"

"We've got to see this!" I exclaimed. "Earth's whole future is at stake!"

"Follow me!" exclaimed Stan, running for the park entrance.

I admit it. I was a little nervous. After all, how safe could it be for fourth graders to be wandering around New York City in the middle of the night? But even getting mugged didn't seem that bad compared with the whole planet being turned inside out. So I gritted my teeth and followed Stan.

We ran through dark and deserted streets, and then Stan turned the corner into Times

Square. We stopped in our tracks.

Thousands of flashing lights and glowing signs made the city bright as day. People packed the streets. Cars and taxis jammed the roadway. Here it was, one o'clock in the morning. But in Times Square, it might as well have been high noon!

Stan climbed onto a bench. From there, he swung himself over to a streetlight, where he began to shinny up the pole.

I was astonished. "What are you doing?"

Suspended above the crowd, Stan hung on with one arm. That left his other hand free to get a finger up his nose. "I, Stan, am programming my nasal processor to deflect the signal from Lower East Hoola Moola over to the TV."

I looked around desperately. *"What* TV?"

Then I saw it—mounted halfway up a building—the giant Times Square JumboTron, the largest TV screen in New York!

NOW I SEE THE big PICTURE.

# Chapter 16
# THE ICE CREAM FLOATS

Suddenly, there it was, right on the Times Square JumboTron—the island of Lower East Hoola Moola. Palm trees, sandy beaches, sparkling ocean, bright sunshine—

"But it's the middle of the night!" I protested.

"It's the middle of the night *here*!" Stan corrected me. "Hoola Moolan time is twelve hours ahead of New York. It's one o'clock in the afternoon there."

The Candy Land game was set up on a table on the beach. General Put-On, who was still mounted on Monty, the fire-breathing ostrich, pored over the board in intense concentration. Opposite him, Ra'at A. Tooey was perched atop a pyramid of coconuts.

The general picked a card—double blue. He

moved his gingerbread game piece to the second blue square, and punched the time clock. In the grandstand of bleachers, thousands of GI Pants cheered. A reporter from ESPN—Extremely Sporting Pants Network—jabbered excitedly into a microphone. An aide ran up to wipe the sweat off the general's medals, while another rearranged the stars on his shoulders into new and exciting constellations. Monty let fly with an enormous belch, which set the game board on fire. Instantly, a team of Fire Pants burst through the crowd to put out the blaze with their Panty Hose.

**"You call yourself a Candy Land player?"** Ra'at A. Tooey sneered right in General Put-On's face. **"You don't know the Peanut Brittle House from the Gumdrop Mountains!** My great-grandmother could beat you with four hands tied behind her back!"

"What's he trying to do?" I called up to Stan. "He's getting the general mad at him!"

"Well, he *is* a Ra'at," Stan reminded me. "You have to expect a certain amount of trash talk."

Ra'at A. Tooey was next. He picked a card

and flashed it for all to see. It was the Ice Cream Floats, the best card in all of Candy Land. It allows you to advance your gingerbread man to the Ice Cream Floats space—nine-tenths of the way to the Candy Castle! It was almost a sure win.

Na-Na-Na-Na. . .
Hey, hey, hey!
Good-bye!

"All right, Ra'at!" I cheered. This rodent was a Candy Land superstar! Earth's safety was in the bag!

I wasn't counting on one thing—General Put-On's famous temper.

*"Aw, twill!!!"* he howled, picking

up the whole table and hurling it into the ocean. ***"Twill! Twill! Twill!"*** He jumped down from his mount and started kicking vast clouds of sand in all directions. Then he pulled a huge clove of garlic out of his uniform pocket and fed it to Monty.

*"Ohhhhhhhh, no!"*

There was a mad scramble as the entire platoon of GI Pants dove off the bleachers into the safety of the ocean.

A split second later, Monty let fly an enormous belch. The grandstand was engulfed in flames.

But the red-faced general didn't even seem to notice. He kicked over the pyramid of coconuts, sending his opponent flying. Then he grabbed poor Ra'at A. Tooey in midair and shook him by his tail.

I stared at the JumboTron screen. Hidden Candy Land cards were falling out of the Ra'at's fur and fluttering to the beach. They were all Ice Cream Floats.

The general raised an eyebrow. He said, "I smell a rat."

"You mean you smell a *Ra'at!*" the Rodentian corrected hastily. "Sorry, General. It was a long flight. Maybe I should take a shower. Nobody likes a dirty Ra'at."

General Put-On flew into a blind rage. *"Cheater!"* he bellowed. ***"Arrest this rodent!"***

A siren cut the air as sentry Pants came from all directions.

"Stan!" I called. "What's the penalty on Pan for cheating at Candy Land?"

"Six millennia of hard labor," came the reply. "But with good behavior, he might cut it down to four."

"This is our fault!" I cried.

If I'd learned anything from Stan Mflxnys, it was that all life forms are important—even slimy and disgusting ones like Ra'at A. Tooey. I wouldn't pick the guy to have tea with the Queen of England, but we had to save him from General Put-On.

# Chapter 17
# SAVE OUR SEAMS

Halfway up the streetlight, Stan put his finger to his nostril. "This is a Stitch-in-Time distress call for General Put-On! S.O.S.—save our seams!"

On the JumboTron, General Put-On reached up for his nasal processor and dropped the Ra'at.

"Run!" I howled at the screen.

Did he ever! The Rodentian's short legs were already pumping when he hit the sand. He made a sprint that would have left any NFL halfback green with envy. GI Pants dove at him every which way; nose computers shot lightning bolts at him. He dodged it all. The intergalactic traveler leaped into his plane and rocketed into the sky a split second before Monty barbecued the runway.

"Phew!" I let my breath out. "Man, that was close!"

Stan climbed down the pole. The picture from Lower East Hoola Moola disappeared from the JumboTron as soon as his finger left his nose.

We walked around for another hour, but Stan's Pan-tastic alien-life-form detector kept cutting in and out. So we had no chance of tracking down any Humongans. Eventually we just returned to Central Park and crawled back into the tent for a few hours' sleep.

In the morning, Mr. Slomin announced that the class would be touring Greenwich Village, going to a virtual-reality video arcade, and taking a ride on the Staten Island Ferry past the Statue of Liberty. He said it to everybody, but he was looking straight at Stan and me, trying to rub it in that we wouldn't get to go.

But today, Mr. Slomin threw us a curve ball. *He* would be taking the class on the bus; we were to be left with Mrs. Ford. I must have looked relieved, because he added, "If Mrs. Ford has anything to report about you two, you'll both have a month of detentions when we get back home."

"I'd be overjoyed to serve a month of detentions," I whispered to Stan, "if there's going to be an Earth to serve them on."

The class drove off, cheering and pounding on the windows of the bus. We were left to clean up the mess from breakfast. Mrs. Ford set us to work, then sat down on a campstool to do her needlepoint. Our bus driver set two stitches in a pink rose, and fell fast asleep.

> What a SPINE-TINGLING hObby!

"Stan!" I hissed. "Let's get out of here!"

He looked shocked. "But we'll be punished!"

"The whole planet's going to be punished if we can't find those Humongans! Come on!"

I tossed a plate of half-eaten bagels into the wire trash bin.

"Hey, what's the big idea? Can't a Ra'at enjoy his breakfast in peace?"

# Chapter 18
# THANKS FOR NOTHING

Stan and I both gawked. There was a rat in the garbage, chowing down on what was left of a honey bun. Not just a normal rat, but Ra'at A. Tooey himself, back from the island of Lower East Hoola Moola.

So help me, I was so glad to see the little guy alive and well, I reached down to pull him out of there. But he batted my hand away with a swipe of his tail.

"You again!" he snarled, beady eyes blazing. "Thanks for nothing, pal!"

"Hey," I said sharply. "If it wasn't for us, you'd still be under arrest. At least we got out of there."

"Yeah, sure!" the Rodentian exclaimed sarcastically. "Real quality transportation. That so-called airplane you got me ran out of juice over a split-level in New Jersey. Lucky for me those people had a trampoline in their backyard, or I'd be one dead Ra'at!"

"I, Stan, should have used a few thousand extra batteries while I had Stone Cold Steve Austin to carry them," my exchange buddy admitted. "My nasal processor has become very weak."

Shoulda, coulda, woulda . . .

The Rodentian looked disgusted. "Now he tells me. Listen, pal, we Ra'ats have some of the most advanced technology in the Cheesy Way galaxy. But on our own, we're pretty much left with scurrying. Ever try to scurry through the Lincoln Tunnel at rush hour? Those bus drivers have no respect for a long tail."

Band-Aids were wrapped all the way down the rear part of the thin tail. "Ouch," I said sympathetically.

"Tell me about it," he grumbled. "And I finally limp into New York with my caboose flattened by a twenty-ton bus just in time to wave good-bye to the spaceship that's supposed to be my ride home. This happens to us Ra'ats *every time*!"

We go out of our way to help you nonrodent life forms. But we always end up getting treated like vermin!"

I felt guilty. "Well, couldn't you call for another ship?"

"Listen, bub," he sneered, "catching a spaceship to the Cheesy Way galaxy isn't like getting on a bus to Brooklyn. If you miss a flight to Rodentia Alpha, you've got a heck of wait till the next one." He climbed out of the can. "Here, give me a hand with my luggage."

This turned out to be a dirty, crumpled Ziploc sandwich bag. Inside were half a jelly bean, a chewed pen cap, a mud-encrusted subway token, a chicken bone, a linty Gummi Bear, and a gleaming bright green Statue of Liberty key chain. "Souvenirs for the grandkids," he told me.

HE's a Rat Packer.

Stan came over and held out his pinkie. "On behalf of the Pan-Pan Travel Bureau, I, Stan, would like to apologize for the terrible situation we've put you in."

Ra'at A. Tooey reached up and shook it. "I'm not a Ra'at who holds a grudge," he sighed. "You want my advice? Save yourself. I was there when Omega Twelve got turned inside out. Upside-down buildings everywhere—it took me a month to get the mud out of my ears! And dark! Just try to read a street sign! If it wasn't for that electric toothbrush, I never would have dug my way out! If I were you, I'd be long gone by the time noon rolls around."

"You mean midnight," I corrected. "That's

when they're turning us inside out. Midnight."

The Ra'at shrugged. "If you say so, pal. But the word on the street is it's going to happen at noon. And we Ra'ats are never wrong about the word on the street."

I glared down at him. "I was at the UN when they played the video. I heard General Put-On with my own ears. He said *midnight*."

All at once, Stan's eyes widened in horror. "Midnight *Hoola Moolan time*!" he exclaimed. "That's twelve hours *earlier* than here! Devin, he's right—it *is* noon!"

"But that's only three hours away!" I croaked, my blood chilling to ice water.

Ra'at A. Tooey dumped out his Ziploc bag and began sorting through his treasures on the grass. "Maybe I can trade some of this stuff for a grapefruit. **When a planet gets turned inside out, vitamin C is almost impossible to come by**."

Stan picked up the shiny key chain. "The Statue of Liberty," he sighed. "It's known throughout the galaxy. I, Stan, really wanted to see it."

I wasn't in the mood. "Don't even think about it. We've got less than three hours to find those giant green robots. We don't have time for a giant green statue."

We stood there staring at each other, taking in what I'd just said. It was almost a silent instant replay.

And suddenly, the answer seemed so obvious that it was crazy we hadn't figured it out days ago!

Ra'at A. Tooey stared blankly at us. "Am I missing something?"

How could a two-hundred-foot green robot hide in New York City? By impersonating a two-hundred-foot green statue.

# Chapter 19
# DESTINATION: DOWNTOWN

Of course! The Humongan was on a giant pedestal in New York harbor, posing as the Statue of Liberty!

"Call General Put-On!" I crowed. "Tell him we've figured out who's tapping the Crease!"

> ELEMENTARY, MY dear RaT-SON!

Stan put his finger up his nose. I waited. Nothing happened.

"Uh-oh," the Ra'at said gravely.

"We'll find some batteries," I promised.

Stan shook his head. "That isn't the problem. I, Stan, believe that General Put-On has already begun warming up the Planetary Mega-Gravitron. That would block all messages coming into Lower East Hoola Moola."

"But how can we reach him?" I asked.

"We can't," Stan replied. "We must approach the Humongan directly and convince him to release his hold on the Crease."

**"In other words,"** groaned Ra'at A. Tooey, **"we have to *talk* to the Statue of Liberty."**

"It's worth a try," Stan said seriously. "Humongans are renowned throughout this galaxy for their reasonableness."

"Well, what are we waiting for?" The Rodentian scampered up the side of my exchange buddy's pant leg and plopped himself in his shirt pocket.

With a quick check to make sure Mrs. Ford was still asleep, we sprinted out of the park and jumped into a taxi.

"Statue of Liberty!" I barked at the driver.

He eyed us in his rearview mirror. "That's an expensive ride from here, kid. Sure you've got enough money?"

Whoops.

Stan spoke up. "Would you consider accepting an invisible interstellar payment voucher, backed by the good credit of his Most Tailored Majesty, the Grand Pant himself?"

Uh . . . Sure!

He kicked us out of the cab.

"Funny," Stan mused. "Usually, the Grand Pant's name opens doors all over the universe."

"The subway!" I yowled, pulling Stan toward the entrance. "We've got enough money for that!"

The New York City subway system is a crazy

thing. Even Stan, whose travel agent work had taken him all over the galaxy, couldn't figure it out. The map showed dozens of multicolored train lines crisscrossing each other like spaghetti.

LOOKS MOrE LiKE LiNquiNi TO ME. Or MaybE aNqEL hair.

We did *everything* wrong. We went uptown when we needed to go downtown. We took the local when we wanted the express. We blundered through the exit door and had to pay again. When we finally got ourselves turned around, somehow we ended up on a train bound for Brooklyn.

I looked at my watch. It was eleven o'clock. "We've wasted almost *two hours!*" I glared at the tiny head poking out of Stan's shirt pocket. "I thought you said Ra'ats use the subway all the time!"

"I said *rats* use the subway all the time!" he retorted. **"We Ra'ats like to travel first class."**

I wanted to cry. There was no way we'd ever make it now.

And then a kind voice behind us said, "Statue of Liberty? Take the A train to Fifty-ninth

Street, and switch to the downtown Number One to South Ferry. That's where you get the boat for the Statue of Liberty."

I turned to look at the lady who had helped us, but she had already walked on past, her high heels clicking on the platform. I wanted to thank her. Maybe even tell her that she might have just saved the planet. But our train pulled up and we had to get on.

My exchange buddy was impressed too. "I, Stan, have witnessed many amazing things in my travels with the Pan-Pan Travel Bureau. I have watched the legendary evaporating pachyderms of Sirius trumpet proud blasts with their trunks and disappear into wisps of gray mist. I have heard the complaining of the famous disgruntled miners of the Coal Sack. I have looked on as the tireless moose-antlered hummingbirds of Antares have flapped valiantly in a vain attempt to keep their forty-pound heads aloft. But we have just seen one of the rarest and most wondrous creatures in the galaxy."

"What's that?" I asked.

"The friendly New Yorker."

# Chapter 20

# A KING·SIZE NASAL PROCESSOR

Eleven-fifteen. Eleven-thirty . . .

I gritted my teeth and tried to will our train to go faster. Every station stop seemed like an endless delay. I was a one-kid sweat bath by the time we pulled in to South Ferry.

Stan and I ran down the platform.

"Get out of the way!" Ra'at A. Tooey barked at the passengers ahead of us.

"What's the matter?" I said to a shocked man as we brushed past him on the stairs. **"Haven't you ever seen a talking rat before?"**

By now the sun was high in the sky, and the New York harbor gleamed like a sea of diamonds. As stressed out as I was, I couldn't help noticing the pure *energy* of the place—the towering skyline, the rush of people and cars, and even the boats on the water. In Battery Park, the southern tip of Manhattan island, a real Hollywood film crew was shooting a movie. I stared. Behind the camera was none other than Steven Spielberg, the most famous movie director of all time.

The Ra'at pointed. "Look!"

We followed his beady-eyed gaze. There, across the harbor, stood the Statue of Liberty. If there was ever any doubt that it was the source of the power drain, it was gone now. **Miss Liberty was holding the tip of her torch up her nose!**

"Brilliant," breathed Stan. "The Crease energy is being diverted to a king-size nasal processor."

"Is that a Humongan?" I asked.

Stan put a finger in his nostril. "Impossible to tell. My Pan-tastic alien life form detector is completely off-line. It's definitely an imposter, though. This creature is one hundred sixty feet tall. The actual Statue of Liberty should only be one hundred fifty-one feet."

I was confused. "But I thought Humongans

were supposed to be two hundred feet tall."

"This must be a very short Humongan," Stan decided.

**"An unhumongous Humongan,"** groaned Ra'at A. Tooey. **"What will they think of next?"**

"Okay," I said. "There's the ticket window for Liberty Island."

The line stretched as far as I could see. We ran

to take our place behind the last person. There, a small sign declared: FROM THIS POINT, THE WAIT IS APPROXIMATELY TWO HOURS.

"Two hours?" I cried. "We've only got twenty minutes!"

"Devin! Stan!" came a familiar voice. "What are you guys doing here?"

> And you thought Space Mountain was bad.

I wheeled around. Tanner Phelps was at the cotton candy stand. Behind him, I could see our entire class waiting at the entrance to the Staten Island Ferry.

"Duck!" I whispered to the Ra'at.

"Where?!" he asked excitedly.

"Get *down*!" Stan commanded.

The Rodentian was disappointed. "Too bad. Du'ucks are the greatest troubleshooters in the universe. There is no problem so large that a du'uck won't take a quack at it." And he disappeared inside Stan's shirt pocket.

"Tanner, keep your voice down!" I hissed at our classmate. "If Mr. Slomin sees us, we're cooked!"

"Where's Mrs. Ford?" he asked.

"Still in Central Park," I admitted. "Listen, Tanner, we need to sneak onto the ferry with you guys. It's our only chance to get close to the Statue of Liberty."

Tanner grinned with every tooth in his head. "What's in it for me?"

"My basketball card collection," I offered. "No? What if I throw in my Niagara Falls paperweight?"

He smiled even wider. "Not enough."

I wanted to punch the guy. All life on Earth could get squashed because this big jerk got his jollies by busting our chops.

And then Stan Mflxnys—the guy who thought traffic jams and dentist appointments were big-time entertainment—came up with exactly the right thing to say.

"How about two free tickets the next time Wrestlemania comes to Clearview? Plus backstage passes to meet Stone Cold Steve Austin."

All at once, the smirk disappeared from Tanner's face.

## Chapter 21

# TAKE ME TO THE HENHOUSE

Mr. Slomin stood by the door counting heads as we filed onto the Staten Island Ferry. I followed close behind Tanner, my face practically buried in the hood of his jacket. Stan was sandwiched so tightly between Ralph and Joey that I think they carried him most of the way.

"That's funny," murmured Mr. Slomin when we were all on board and the ferry had left the dock. "I'm coming up with two *more* kids than I brought."

"You musta double-counted a couple of 'em." The conductor shrugged. "Happens all the time."

The teacher shook his head. "Weirdest field trip I've ever been on. We're supposed to be at Calhoun Gorge, you know."

Stan and I broke from the class and took the stairs two at a time to the top deck.

The Statue of Liberty was a few hundred yards away and getting closer.

"Can you use your nasal processor to talk to the Humongan?" I asked urgently.

Stan put his finger up his nose. "Negative. All communication functions have shut down. I, Stan, must perform a system diagnostic."

I stared at him. "You mean the egg thing? *Now?* I can't believe you remembered to bring one along on this wild goose chase!"

"I didn't bring one," my exchange buddy informed me. "I, Stan, will have to lay my own."

"What? *Here?*"

"Certainly not," Stan said primly. "A Pant needs privacy. **Egg-laying is a very personal thing.** Take me to the henhouse."

"The *henhouse?*" I repeated. "What are you, nuts? We're on a boat to Staten Island! There isn't any henhouse!"

We finally decided on the bathroom. It was a little cramped in there, but it was the only privacy on the crowded ferry. I stood guard outside. Even though ☞ **Rule 7:** was *Listen to music; listen to reason; but never listen in on some poor guy in the bathroom*, I couldn't help positioning my ear up against the door. I have no idea what I expected to hear.

First there was a rustling sound, like a chicken resettling its feathers. That was followed by a soft clucking in a voice I recognized as Stan's.

Joey Petrillo came strolling down the deck. "Hi, Devin. Is that Stan in there?"

I was about to say yes when a series of sharp squawks rang out from inside the bathroom.

I'll bet my face was red as a tomato. I mean, I'd put up with a lot of humiliating uncoolness from Stan Mflxnys. Sometimes it felt like I spent half my life explaining away every dweeby thing he did. That's not even including his nasal processor, which made him come off as the biggest nose picker of all time. But this—*this* was beyond anything!

"That's not Stan," I said quickly. "It's—uh—some other guy."

At that moment, Stan said in his normal voice, "Eureka, Devin. The shell has appeared."

"Cluck harder," suggested Ra'at A. Tooey.

And the squawking started up again.

Joey rolled his eyes. **"Well, that chicken sure does a great impression of Stan."** And he ran off, calling, "Hey, Tanner! Stan's in the bathroom with some dude! And he's pretending to be a chicken!"

After what seemed like forever, my exchange

buddy burst out of the bathroom, the soft-boiled egg in his hand. I'd never seen him so depressed.

"Three minutes!" he cried. "It took three full minutes to cook this! Do you know what that means? The power drain from the Crease has gotten so severe that my nasal processor is no stronger than a common egg cooker! Soon the energy level will be down to zero!"

I looked over the railing of the ferry. The Statue of Liberty was fifty yards away. It would never get any closer than this.

"What are we going to do?" demanded Ra'at A. Tooey. "If there's one thing we Ra'ats can't stand, it's wasting time. It comes from running down the street with the exterminator on your tail."

"There is only one possible course of action," my exchange buddy decided. "I, Stan, must blow my nose."

"You don't even have a Kleenex," I moaned.

USE aN air haNKY!

"Blowing your nose is a special emergency function of the nasal processor," he explained. "A

Pant is able to fire off all the remaining power in his nose in one final blast of energy. That just might be enough to launch us off this boat and get us close enough to talk to the Humongan."

Suddenly, an angry voice boomed, "Devin! Stan! What are you doing here? **What have**

*you done with Mrs. Ford?"*

I spun around. Mr. Slomin was pushing through the crowd, his face an unhealthy shade of purple.

I checked my watch. It was ten minutes to twelve. Earth wouldn't make it through another chewing out by Mr. Slomin. Whatever we did, it had to be *fast!*

But how could we try anything with our teacher standing right there? "If only there was some way to create a diversion," I mumbled aloud.

"A diversion?" The Ra'at pulled himself upright in Stan's pocket. "Bub, if there's one thing we Ra'ats know how to do, it's create diversions! One diversion, coming up."

He bellowed, **"Look! A rat! A rat!"** Then he jumped down to the deck of the ferry and darted around the passengers' feet, slapping at ankles with his bandaged tail.

Pandemonium broke loose. A cry of "Ra-a-a-at!!" went up like an air raid siren. People were running and jumping and screaming. Some vaulted up on benches. Others tried to beat off the Rodentian with coats and brief-cases.

Best of all, Mr. Slomin totally disappeared in the crazy crowd. The coast was clear!

"Do it, Stan!" I urged. "Blow your nose!"

# Chapter 22

# CUTTER, CUTTER, PEANUT BUTTER

The last thing I remember was Stan with a finger plugging each nostril. His face turned red. His cheeks puffed out from the effort of his blowing. And then everything went nuts.

With a loud hissing sound, dense white mist encircled Stan and me like a thick fog. A powerful force picked me up by the seat of my jeans and lifted me clear out of the boat. Through the air I sailed, the waters of New York Harbor sparkling below.

"I hope you know how to land!" I called over at Stan, who was beside me.

He looked completely blank. "Land?"

*Wham!*

We came down in a small grove of juniper bushes. My clothes were torn, and I was scratched and bleeding by the time we managed to crawl out.

We looked up. There, right above us, loomed the "statue." I cupped my hands to my mouth. "Hey, you!" I bellowed. "Humongan! Down here!"

"It's no use," decided Stan. "We'll have to take the staircase up to the crown."

"Aren't you forgetting something?" I reminded him. "The *real* statue has a staircase. This isn't the real statue; it's an alien."

"Humongans started out as robots," Stan explained. "Their makers needed a way to get around inside their creations. So they installed stairs. And even though Humongans now are born and grow up like other life forms, staircases continue to be part of their bodies."

Sure enough, there it was—the entrance to the steps. There was a velvet rope at the door. A long line of people stretched down the path. I checked my watch. Eight minutes to go! We'd never make it if we had to wait.

I cried, *"Cutter, cutter, peanut butter!"* and the two of us barreled in to the head of the line. Then came the climbing—160 feet straight up a narrow, dark, steep, hot, cramped staircase, pushing past flocks of sweaty tourists the whole way.

"Excuse me . . . coming through . . . planetary emergency . , , excuse me . . ."

It was a major workout. I was drenched by the time we made it to the giant alien's kneecap. At belly button level, some little kid didn't want to let me by. When I pushed past him, he started shrieking. So much for ☛ **Rule 36: Keep a low profile.** The noise echoed all the way up and down the steps. I thought I was going to bust an eardrum!

NO pain, NO gain.

We were both exhausted by the time we made it to the top. I looked out the opening in the "statue's" crown. All of New York lay before us.

"Hey, Humongan!" I rasped with what was left of my breath. "Listen up!"

"Devin! Shhh!" Stan whispered. "Is that any way to speak to the most mature and reasonable species in the galaxy?" He cleared his throat and addressed the alien that was all around us.

"Pardon me, your Great and Extremely Enormous Massiveness. I am Agent Mflxnys of the Pan-Pan Travel Bureau, sometimes known as Stan. Might I take a tiny moment of your sizably vast, and hugely valuable time?"

I held my breath. Earth's whole future depended on what happened right now.

At first there was total silence except for the distant screaming of that little kid on the stairs.

Then a voice that came from all around us boomed, *"WHADDAYA WANT?"*

"Well, Your Largeness," Stan began, "you know how you've been tapping energy out of the Crease?"

*"YEAH?"* The voice was so loud I could almost feel it rattling my brain. *"SO?"*

"So I, Stan, was wondering if you could—well, you know—cut it out?"

There was the creaking of metal as the statue's giant brow furrowed. The Humongan was thinking it over!

*"NO!"* resounded our answer at last.

"No?" I repeated. "What do you mean, no? The whole future of the planet is riding on this!"

I'm pretty sure the Humongan frowned, because the ground bent under our feet, forming a little gully directly above the bridge of the "statue's" nose. Stan and I both lost our balance and conked heads.

*"FINDERS KEEPERS, LOSERS WEEPERS!!"* thundered the Humongan. *"YOU SNOOZE, YOU LOSE, PAL!!"*

*This* was the most mature species in the

galaxy? This guy reminded me of Lindsay!

My exchange buddy was genuinely bewildered. "I, Stan, don't understand it. Humongans are renowned for their reasonableness."

"Yeah, well, are you sure this is a real Humongan? This guy's about as reasonable as my rotten sister! Plus he's forty feet shorter than he's supposed to be. . . ."

# Chapter 23
# A NOT·SO·LITTLE BRAT

When it finally dawned on me, it was like a brilliant sunrise. I dragged Stan back to his feet by his polka-dot tie. *"That's it!"*

Stan looked blank. "You have information, Devin?"

I practically screamed it in his face. "This *is* a real Humongan! But it's just a kid! That's why he's too short—he's not fully grown yet! And he talks like my sister because he's going through a *phase!*"

Stan was amazed. "So you're saying that tapping the Crease is nothing more than—"

"Misbehavior!" I cried. "He's being *bad!*"

It was mind-blowing! Half a world away, a maniac on an ostrich was about to turn Earth inside out. Pan was going crazy. The whole galaxy was on high alert. And it was all because of one rotten kid!

This was like a five-year-old who digs up an anthill in his backyard. Does he ever think how the ants must feel? Of course not! He's just playing around!

That's what the Humongan was doing—playing! And we were the ants, about to lose our home—all six billion of us!

"If only I, Stan, had the enormous brainpower of a Smarty-Pant," my exchange buddy lamented. "Mr. Know-It-All would see what to do."

I was triumphant. "What do you do with a naughty kid? Tattle on him to his parents! I'll bet they're worried sick about this not-so-little brat!"

"But my nasal processor is stone dead!" Stan protested. "We have no way to send a message through deep space!"

I checked my watch. Two minutes to go. It was so frustrating I wanted to scream. We were totally out of power. Yet, just a few yards below us, the Humongan's torch was tapped into the greatest energy source in the whole universe!

I got an idea. I grabbed Stan and pushed him out the crown of the "statue," leaving him hanging on to one of the iron slats.

"Devin, what are you *doing*?" he hissed at me. "Without my nasal processor, I, Stan, will be killed if I fall!"

"Just hang in there!" I urged. Then I ran to the stairs and cried. "Help! Help! My friend went over the side! Quick! Give me your belts so we can pull him back in!"

It's amazing how fast cranky tourists can turn into a rescue squad. In a few seconds, I had twenty belts tied together and just as many volunteers ready to yank Stan back up to safety. I took the position at the front of the "rope" so I could block the others from seeing what we were really up to.

Stan grabbed hold of the first belt, but I instructed the men to keep lowering. I watched him climb down the face of the Humongan, rappelling against "Miss Liberty's" forehead like a mountaineer. When he was at the point where the torch was touching the Humongan's nose, I yelled, "Steady!"

My volunteers held fast. At the end of all those belts hung my exchange buddy, high above Liberty Island. His rope arm rested on the big green torch. The other was in its usual position, with Stan's finger up his nose.

He had done it! He was tapped into the Crease! But would the Humongan's parents get the message in time?

I looked at my watch. *Less than a minute to noon!*

AND a NEW YORK MINUTE at that!

## Chapter 24
# OOPS!

All at once, one of my volunteers pointed. "Look! Up in the sky!"

"It's a bird!"

"It's a plane!"

**"It's a giant chocolate-chip cookie!"**

A giant chocolate-chip cookie? Then I remembered. A Humongan ship!

"Stan, you did it!" I called. "They're here!"

Stan shinnied up the belts, and the men hauled him back into the crown.

"We're glad you're alive, son," one of the men said emotionally, choking back tears. "We thought you were a goner there and—*ugggh! Get your finger out of your nose!*"

I couldn't believe it. The Humongans were

here! But it was half a minute to noon!

The Humongan ship hovered low over New York Harbor for a moment. Then it disappeared under the water. After a few seconds, there was a titanic splash and a pair of two-hundred-foot-tall green robots arose from the waves.

"What the—" breathed the man who had pulled Stan inside.

"It's two more statues of liberty!" exclaimed another volunteer. "And they're *alive*!"

*"MOMMY?"* boomed the guilty voice of our Humongan. *"DADDY?"*

I checked my watch. Five seconds to go! Four . . . three . . .

*"DEAR ONE,"* thundered the mother robot, *"HAVE YOU BEEN A NAUGHTY LITTLE HU-MONGAN AGAIN?"*

Two . . . one . . . zero! Oh, no! I put my hands over my head and waited to be crushed like a bug.

And just like that, the Humongan took the torch out of his nose. *"I DIDN'T DO IT, MOMMY!"* he whined. *"IT WASN'T ME! IT MUST HAVE BEEN SOMEBODY ELSE! NO-*

*FAIR-NO-FAIR-NO-FAIR-NO-FAIR-NO-FAIR!"*

Stan put his finger in his nostril. "Devin, it's Mr. Know-It-All! The hold on the Crease has been completely released!"

"You mean Earth won't have to be turned inside out?" I cried.

Stan nodded, beaming. "The Grand Pant has ordered the unfastening of the Big Zipper! General Put-On is feeding Monty Alka-Seltzer to soothe his stomach. The emergency is over!"

☞ **Rule 1:** Don't ever act excited—even when you're excited.

Well, who cares about Rule 1 when the planet's just been saved? I threw my arms over my head and started yahooing like a maniac. *"We did it! We did it! We—"*

And then everything tilted crazily this way and that. Stan, the volunteers, and I were tossed around like chicken pieces in a Shake 'n Bake bag. Outside, New York bounced wildly. My first thought was that crazy General Put-On was turning Earth inside out anyway. But then I realized what was actually happening.

Our Humongan had jumped off the Statue of

Liberty's pedestal, and was trying to run away from his parents!

*"Abandon statue!"* I bellowed.

That isn't exactly easy to do when the "statue" is moving. I think I fell down about half the stairs. And I had it easy. Picture what it was like for the families with baby strollers, or the teenagers with heavy backpacks. If Stan hadn't used his nasal processor to help, it would have been a total wipeout. As it was, Stan and I sprinted out of there just a second before the Humongan parents got hold of their naughty child.

"Ha!" I shook my fist up at him. "Now you're going to get it, you big baby!"

I had revenge in my heart. I was psyched for the great granddaddy of all spankings—it has to be heavy duty when the spankers are both two hundred feet tall. But I guess Humongans don't believe in that. Instead, they gave their kid a time-out—right at the top of a fifty-story office tower. While he was up there sulking, they fished the real Statue of Liberty out of New York Harbor. The "dad" carefully shook off the mud and seaweed, and placed Miss Liberty back on her

pedestal. Then the two giant robots turned to face the city skyline. *"WE APOLOGIZE FOR ANY INCONVENIENCE OUR CHILD MAY HAVE CAUSED THIS PLANET!"* boomed the "mom." *"AS WE SAY ON OUR HUMONGAN HOME WORLD, 'OOPS!'"*

And with that, they got their rotten kid down off the skyscraper, summoned their spacecraft up out of the water, and took off, towing Junior's smaller ship behind them. Then, just as they were about to pass over the Staten Island Ferry, they came to a dead stop in midair. There they hovered, just above the boat's top deck.

I squinted into the brilliant sky. "What's going on?"

A tourist standing next to me had a pair of binoculars. "It looks like they're picking up a hitchhiker—very short, kind of furry, long tail—" She made a face. "Oh, yuck, I think it's a *rat*!"

"Of course!" Stan exclaimed. "The Humongan home world lies in exactly the same direction as the Cheesy Way galaxy. The Humongans have volunteered to give Ra'at A. Tooey a lift." He beamed. "Have you ever seen such reasonable life forms?"

I was ready to strangle him. Reasonable? The whole planet came within a heartbeat of total disaster, and all those monsters had to say for themselves was "Oops"? Not to mention that half of New York City had ground to a halt to stare at the sight of giant robots punishing their kid atop a hundred-plus-story building. Why, the only people anywhere who weren't staring pop-eyed at the spectacle in the harbor were Steven Spielberg and his movie crew. They just kept on filming through the whole thing, like this was a typical day at the office.

I guess the famous director was following
☛ **Rule 16:** The show must go on.

# Chapter 25

# SPECIAL EFFECTS

The end.

Well, not *really*. A whole bunch of stuff happened after that.

Mr. Slomin practically killed us when we met back at the ferry terminal. And Mrs. Ford was so upset at being deserted in Central Park she refused to drive the class home. Our principal had to call on Mr. Slomin's cell phone and offer her a raise before she'd even tell us where she had hidden the keys to the bus. So the trip ended on kind of a downer—at least for everybody who didn't know how Stan and I had saved the world.

Nothing was changed when we got back home. Lindsay was still going through her phase, but it didn't bother me anymore. What did I care if she hogged the TV remote—just so long as nobody was going to turn the planet inside out because of it?

While the family tried to keep up with Lindsay's channel surfing, Stan barked away at Fungus, our cocker spaniel. Stan's nasal processor was equipped with a Pan-Tran translator, so he could speak Dog. He was going over all the highlights of the trip. I knew Fungus was really into the story. He was yipping and woofing through the whole thing.

"What's he saying?" I whispered.

"He believes he could have helped us," Stan translated. "Dogs are very good at handling statues."

**"Dogs are very good at handling fire hydrants,"** I corrected. "One-hundred-sixty-foot statues are a little out of their league."

How do you say "bowwow" in Pant?

Suddenly, Lindsay flipped to a news program. Behind the anchorperson was a graphic of the New York skyline with the words MASS HALLUCINATION written across it.

"Turn it up!" I exclaimed.

". . . there's still no explanation for a very strange sight noticed by several thousand people in New York Harbor yesterday," the lady was saying. "Just after noon, onlookers claim to have witnessed two giant Statues of Liberty giving a slightly smaller Statue of Liberty a time-out atop a skyscraper. After that, all three climbed into two flying chocolate-chip cookies and disappeared. Police are baffled. One boy, however, has a theory."

They cut to their New York reporter in Battery Park, exactly where we had been the day before. Standing right next to her was—-

"Devin!" Mom sat bolt upright on the couch. "That's *you*!"

I remembered giving this interview. But never in a million years did I think it would get on TV all the way back home in Clearview!

"Oh, it was pure special effects," I said on television. "None of it was real. They're shooting a science-fiction movie here. See? There's Steven Spielberg behind the camera."

"But—" My dad was bug-eyed. "But I thought you were at Calhoun Gorge!"

"It's a long story," I admitted.

"That reminds me," my exchange buddy added eagerly. "Along with Devin, I, Stan, have been awarded six months of detentions. It's quite an honor."

Fortunately, my parents were so blown away by the sight of their son on TV, that I didn't have to answer too many questions.

"Hey, Stan," I whispered. "What a lucky break that Steven Spielberg happened to be shooting a movie in New York yesterday. Otherwise,

COMING SOON TO a PLANET NEAR YOU.

we never could have come up with a decent explanation for everything that happened."

"Devin," Stan chided me, "luck had nothing to do with it. As soon as I knew we'd be confronting the Humongan in public, I contacted Splbrgnys and asked him to set up his film crew in Battery Park. It was my last message before my nasal processor lost the power to communicate."

"Splbrgnys?" I repeated. "You mean Steven Spielberg is a *Pant*?"

He shrugged. "You didn't think a mere Earthling could make such great movies, did you? Don't look so shocked, Devin. Where do you think he got all that alien footage for *E. T.*?"

On TV, the reporter was wrapping up my interview. "There you have it, folks. The mass hallucination turns out to be nothing more than special effects for a new Steven Spielberg film." He turned back to me. "Any idea what the movie is going to be called?"

On the screen, I watched myself flash a mischievous grin. "*Invasion of the Nose Pickers.*"